THE NIGHT THE MOON WENT MISSING

BY BRENDAN KEARNEY

At night, Moon shines proudly between constellations of stars.

And every morning, Sun rises and beams so brightly that no one notices Moon any more.

"What a show-off!" Moon huffed, as she watched everyone laughing and playing in the sunshine.

When night came around again, everyone turned their lights off and went to sleep.

"Nobody cares about me!" Moon cried.

But someone did care –
it's just that Moon didn't see her.

Lucy could see Moon from her
bedroom window. "It'll be all right, Moon.
I'll see you tomorrow night!" she yawned
as she jumped into bed.

But the following night Moon was gone. And the night after that.

After a few nights Lucy started to worry. She read the newspapers in horror.

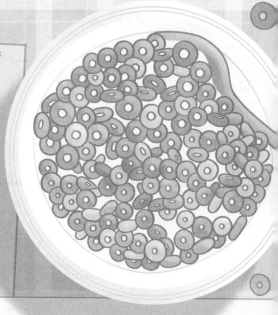

THE EVENING CRESCENT

All the news you need from the surface of the Moon

FREE

WAVE GOODBYE TO YOUR SURFBOARD

Surfers were left very disappointed during the world surf championship this week as the waves were much smaller than expected. The ocean was as flat as a pancake without the gravitational forces from Moon causing big surf. We hope she returns soon!!

More on page 5...

Sales of surfboards have almost halved since the disappearance of Moon. However string sales have gone through the roof as surfers resort to playing conkers until she returns.

THE ☽ LUNAR TIMES

Tuesday morning

Moon news for Planet Earth

MOON LANDING CANCELLE[D]

Moon is missing. Where is she?

When astronauts arrived to land on the surface of the Moon the world was left stunned to find that she had vanished.

Experts are in a state of panic trying to work out where she might be and why she has gone.

Continued on page 6...

Confused astronauts cancel Moon landing as Moon is nowhere to be seen

Have you seen the Moon anywhere? Contact us now if you have.

Eclipse a complete letdown

Thousands of people gathered at the coast to catch a glimpse of the total lunar eclipse but were disappointed when the Moon failed to show.

THE ECLIPSE

KEEPING YOU IN THE DARK SINCE 1886

FREE

The Sun refused to comment.

RABBITS OVERRUN ISLAND!

Predators use the light of the Moon to hunt their prey. Without Moon, rabbits have thrived. So much so in fact, that it is impossible to go anywhere on the island without tripping on a rabbit.

UFO SIGHTINGS AT AN ALL-TIME HIGH

UFO sightings have become more frequent since the weekend, with many blaming the disappearance of the Moon on little green men from Mars.

☆☆ THE ☆☆☆☆☆ ASTRONOMER

The hottest gossip from all your favourite stars

FREE

WINTERS WILL GET COLDER AND COLDER!

We must find Moon before it's too late! Scientists predict our weather will change. If this goes on too long, our summers could get hotter and hotter, and our winters much colder.

MOON CHEESE MINE PLANS IN TATTERS.

Campaigners are delighted that the plans to mine the Moon for cheese have been scrapped. Cheese-lovers, however, are very cheesed off.

Soon panic swept across the world.

People looked everywhere for her.

"Where could she be?" Lucy thought.

The newspaper offered a special reward for whoever found Moon.

Astronomers used huge telescopes to scan the furthest corners of space.

Fearless divers searched the deepest, darkest parts of the ocean.

Explorers even scaled the highest mountains
and trekked through the wildest jungles.

But Moon was nowhere to be found.

Moon had found the perfect hiding place. She felt sad
and more alone than she had ever felt before.

Lucy was feeling lonely, too. Her bedroom was so dark without Moon. "She must be so scared on her own," Lucy thought as she sat awake in bed. "Where could she be?"

Lucy rummaged
under her bed,

searched the attic,

and even checked in the garden shed.
But she found no sign of Moon.

Then she remembered her own favourite hiding spot.
The place she would go to if she was feeling sad or lonely.

Lucy rushed to the end of the garden and scrambled down some steps into a quiet hidden cove.

She noticed a dim glow and was overjoyed to find Moon sitting beside a small pool of water.

"I've found you!" Lucy cheered.

But she could see that Moon wasn't quite so happy.

"What's wrong?" Lucy asked softly.

"Nobody cares about me!" wept Moon. "During the day
everyone is too busy to see me and at night,
when it is my time to shine, people
go inside and ignore me!"

Lucy had an idea. She ran back to the
house and returned a few minutes later.

"Look at this!" Lucy smiled, as she opened the newspaper and began to read aloud.

"Millions search for Moon", "We miss you, Moon!"
"Please come home".

Moon wiped her eyes and smiled at Lucy.

"I can't believe it!" she beamed. "You do care about me!"

"That's right," Lucy replied. "We have all missed you very much. The world is a much darker and scarier place without you."

Suddenly Moon didn't feel so lonely.
"Thank you, Lucy," Moon smiled.

She began to rise above the ocean and
floated through the clouds, back to her
space between the constellations.

By the morning, Lucy was famous.

She was interviewed on TV and in the newspaper,
and the world celebrated the return of Moon.

And a few days later she was presented with
her very special reward...

...a holiday to visit her dear friend Moon in space.

BRENDAN KEARNEY

Brendan Kearney lives and works by the sea in South West England with his family and little dog, Crumble. He has loved drawing since he started scribbling as a child and feels very lucky to be able to draw for a living.

The idea for *The Night the Moon Went Missing* came from a lifelong fascination with space. When Brendan got his first telescope, he started making up stories and saw the Moon and constellations as little characters. He especially liked the animal constellations and would sometimes sit and invent his own. As an adult, these characters and stories often creep into his illustration work and some of them came together as this book. He hopes Lucy is a kind and caring character that children can relate to.

Brendan loves pond dipping and fossil hunting but absolutely hates carrots.

DK | Penguin Random House

Produced for DK by Plum 5 Ltd

Editor Amy Braddon
Designer Brandie Tully-Scott
Consultant Carole Stott
Jacket Coordinator Issy Walsh
Production Editor Abi Maxwell
Production Controller Basia Ossowska
Managing Editor Laura Gilbert
Publishing Manager Francesca Young
Creative Director Helen Senior
Publishing Director Sarah Larter

First published in Great Britain in 2021 by
Dorling Kindersley Limited
DK, One Embassy Gardens, 8 Viaduct Gardens,
London, SW11 7BW

The authorised representative in the EEA is
Dorling Kindersley Verlag GmbH. Arnulfstr. 124,
80636 Munich, Germany

Copyright © 2021 Dorling Kindersley Limited
A Penguin Random House Company
10 9 8 7 6 5 4 3 2
002-323175-Nov/2021

A CIP catalogue record for this book
is available from the British Library.
ISBN: 978-0-2414-8808-9

Printed and bound in the UK

For the curious
www.dk.com

MIX
Paper from
responsible sources
FSC
www.fsc.org
FSC™ C018179

This book was made with Forest
Stewardship Council ™ certified paper –
one small step in DK's commitment to a
sustainable future. For more information
go to www.dk.com/our-green-pledge